DONATELLO

Donatello is the team's brilliant inventor. He can make amazing gadgets, weapons, and vehicles with items scavenged from the trash. Donatello likes order and logic, and he can't stand it when his brothers mess with his stuff.

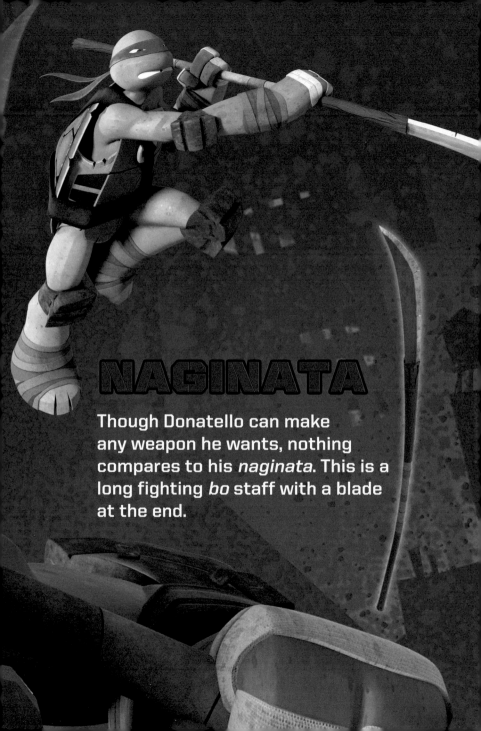

NAGINATA

Though Donatello can make any weapon he wants, nothing compares to his *naginata*. This is a long fighting *bo* staff with a blade at the end.

"I TOTALLY
HAVE TO BUILD
A ROBOT!"

nickelodeon™

TEENAGE MUTANT NINJA TURTLES™

MUTANT ORIGIN:

DONATELLO

Published in the United States by Random House Children's Books,
a division of Random House, Inc., 1745 Broadway, New York, NY 10019,
and in Canada by Random House of Canada Limited, Toronto.
Random House and the colophon are registered trademarks of
Random House, Inc. Nickelodeon, Teenage Mutant Ninja Turtles,
and all related titles, logos, and characters are trademarks of
Viacom International Inc. and Viacom Overseas Holdings C.V.
Based on characters created by Peter Laird and Kevin Eastman.

randomhouse.com/kids

ISBN: 978-0-449-80993-8

Printed in the United States of America
10 9 8 7 6 5 4 3 2 1

nickelodeon.
TEENAGE MUTANT NINJA
TURTLES

MUTANT ORIGIN:

DONATELLO

Adapted by Michael Teitelbaum

Based on the teleplay "Day One, Part Two"
by Joshua Sternin and Jeffrey Ventimilia

RANDOM HOUSE 🏠 NEW YORK

CHAPTER 1

My name is Donatello, but you can call me Donnie.

As Leonardo has been telling you, my brothers and I were inside the hideout of a strange species called the Kraang. We were there to rescue my girlfriend and her father, who is a scientist like me.

Well, okay, she wasn't really my girlfriend—yet. But I was sure that once I learned her name and she got to know me, she would become my girlfriend. I felt it in my bones—we were meant to be together.

At that moment, the four of us were looking down at the inside of the Kraang's hideout. Now, I was pretty familiar with just about every piece of technology humans have ever invented, but the stuff

I was seeing there—wow! This was all super-high-tech alien equipment. It wasn't even vaguely familiar to me.

Kraang guards were patrolling the entire area. We hung on to the rafters and waited for the right time to make our move. When all the guards except two had disappeared, Leonardo and Raphael dropped down and knocked them out.

Leo signaled to Mikey and me to join them. Up close, this place was even more incredible.

"Wow," I said to Raph. "I've never seen anything like this. They're using a metal alloy that even I don't recognize!"

"Gosh," Raph said in that mocking tone he uses whenever I talk tech. "A metal alloy even you don't know about. It boggles the mind!"

I really can't stand it when he talks to me that way. Especially since he doesn't know the first thing about metal alloys.

"Dude, you want to talk metallurgy with me?" I asked, getting up in Raph's face. "Bring it!"

"As a matter of fact, I don't want to have that conversation with you," Raph replied. "And—"

"Guys!" Leonardo interrupted. I could hear the frustration in his voice. "What part of being in an enemy lair do you not understand?"

Leo made a good point. Splinter always talked about ninjas using stealth and silence. I guess Raph and I weren't being too stealthy or silent-y. I had to do a better job of focusing on the task at hand.

We spotted a group of Kraang guards. Using the element of surprise, we easily subdued them. Then we sneaked into another room and got our first close-up look at these dudes.

Holy cow! Mikey was right!

The Kraang weren't wearing suits anymore—in fact, they weren't even wearing skin! Their human appearances had only been a disguise. Underneath they

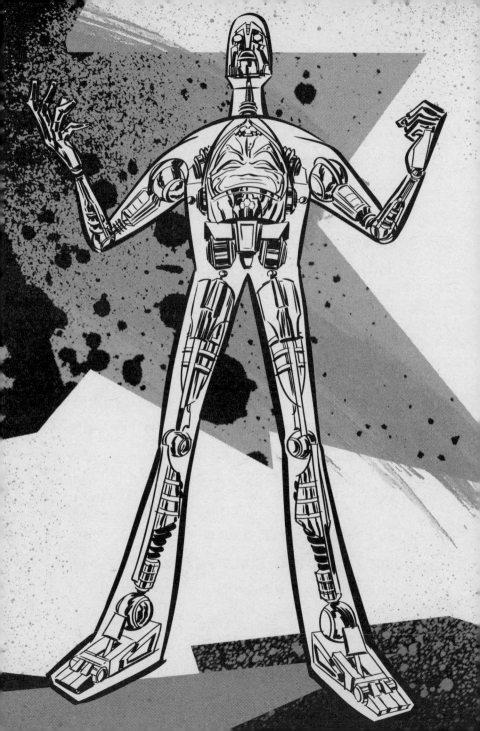

seemed to be cybernetic droids of some sort. I couldn't tell what their blue outer armor was made of, but it was translucent, and I could see the pistons and servo motors working away underneath it. Their eyes were glowing red lights.

Two thoughts hit me instantly: The first was "Wow! I totally have to build a robot when I get back to the lair. And the second was "Mikey was one hundred percent right!"

"Alien robots!" I said. "They really are alien robots!"

"Alien robots, huh?" Mikey said, rubbing his chin. "Now, where have I heard that before? Oh, yeah, I remember. I've only been saying it since the first day we came aboveground!"

The Kraang-droids attacked and we battled them. They fought furiously, blasting their energy weapons, but all our ninja training paid off.

One Kraang-droid had me in his sights. I rolled away, feeling the heat of the explosion on my back. I came up ready to lunge, hoping one good jab of my *bo* staff would get me a better look at his wiring.

The best thing was, we were finally working as a team, taking out the Kraang one by one.

Or so I thought.

I glanced back over my shoulder and

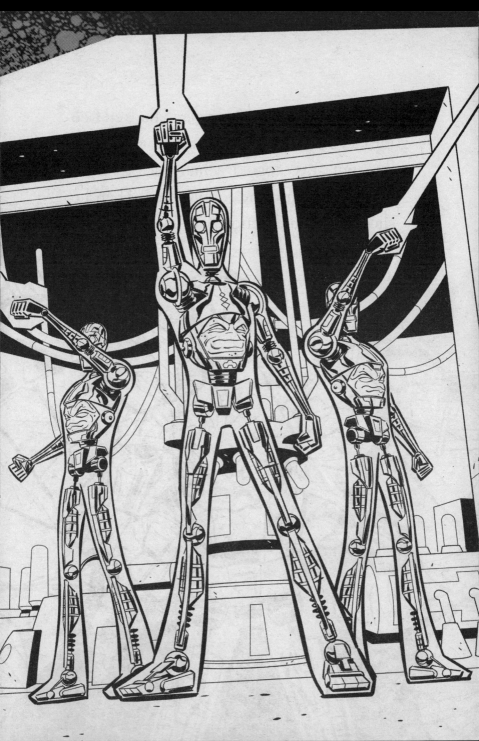

saw that one of the Kraang had backed Leo into a corner. Before I could move to help him out, Leo tossed a handful of blinding powder into the robot's face. Then he sliced at its midsection with his *katana*.

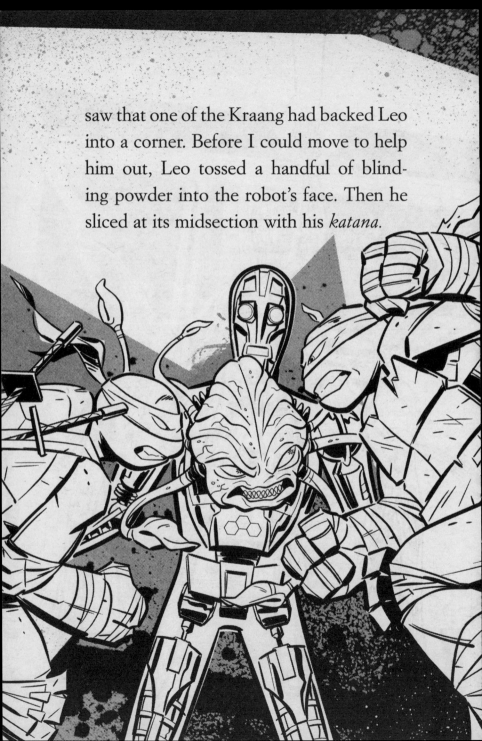

The Kraang-droid tumbled backward and started sparking. Smoke poured from the opening in its belly. And then maybe the strangest thing I'd ever seen happened. No, there's no maybe about it—it was the strangest thing I'd ever seen.

A pink brain with eyes and a mouth and gyrating tentacles slithered out of the opening.

Mikey reacted swiftly. He slammed the brain-thing with his *nunchucks,* stunning it. Then he picked up the slithering, slimy creature by one tentacle and shook it at the rest of us.

"See! See! I told you!" he shouted. "It's a brain-thing. I told you! I told you, but did any of you believe me? Nooooo . . . because you all think I'm just some kind of bonehead!"

That was when the stunned brain-thing woke up. It bit Mikey on the arm.

"Ow!" he cried, flinging the creature off of him.

It flew across the room and slammed into an alarm button, setting off a loud, blaring siren.

Not the best way to prove his point about not being a bone-head, in my humble opinion. My brothers and I all stared at Mikey.

"Okay, I know, bad move, but I was still right about the whole alien robot brain-thing!" he said defensively. "You've gotta give me that!"

Kraang-droids started appearing in every doorway and hall.

"Let's move!" Leonardo ordered.

"Move where?" Raph asked. He had a point. It seemed like the Kraang-droids were everywhere. I looked around, searching for a way out of this. Then I spotted something vaguely familiar overhead.

"I think those are power conduits," I said, looking up at the ceiling.

"That is really interesting," Raphael said, his voice dripping with sarcasm. "Thanks for sharing, Donnie!"

He thought I was just showing off, but he totally missed the point!

"Listen, meathead, the conduits are all converging that way," I explained, pointing to a corner where the pipes disappeared. "Which means that whatever is going on in that direction is important!"

I took off in the direction the conduits were heading. Leonardo ran close behind. Glancing back over my shoulder, I saw Mikey pointing a finger in Raph's face.

"You got spanked by Donnie!" he said, laughing.

Raph didn't answer. He just grabbed Mikey's finger and bent it backward.

"Ow! Ow!" Mikey cried. "Mercy!"

Raph let go of Mikey's finger and the two of them followed us around the corner.

We raced down a hallway with the Kraang-droids right behind us. I spotted a big metal door with a small window and a complex high-tech lock. Peering in the window, I saw . . . her.

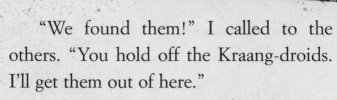

"We found them!" I called to the others. "You hold off the Kraang-droids. I'll get them out of here."

It was my almost, soon-to-be girl-friend, What's-Her-Face. She was with her father, and she was even prettier than I had remembered. I stared at her through the small window in the thick steel door.

"Don't worry," I assured her. "I'll have you out of there in a second!"

"Okay, giant lizard-thing," the girl replied. So she wasn't so clear on our species. I could tell we were totally making progress. This time, she didn't shriek when she saw my face!

"Turtle, actually," I pointed out. "I'm Donatello."

I couldn't believe I was finally getting the chance to introduce myself to her. This was so exciting!

"April," she replied.

April . . . hmmm . . .

"Wow, that's a pretty na—"

Laser pulses bounced off the hallway walls.

"The lock, Donnie!" Leonardo shouted, pressing my face into the glass.

"Right! Sorry! The lock."

I got right to work rewiring the circuitry, but it was slow going. I could hear Mikey attack a line of Kraang-droids with spinning blows from his *nunchucks*. The droids went down like bowling pins. Inside the cell, April was starting to panic.

"Not to rush you or anything," she said, "but hurry up!"

"Hey!" I shot back. "You think it's easy trying to pick a lock with these hands?"

I held up my three thick fingers so April could see them through the glass.

"Oh, sorry," April replied.

Aww, she was so sweet!

Raphael stepped up to the door.

"Oh, for the love of— Get out of my way!" he shouted, shoving me away from the door.

Raphael attacked the electronic lock
with his *sais*. Again and again he jammed the
sharp point into the delicate mechanism.
Sparks flew. But before he could force the

door open, another door at the back of the cell slid back. A group of Kraang-droids grabbed April and her father and dragged them from the cell.

"No! No! Let me go!" April shouted as she disappeared.

Just as Raph finally got the door to open and we raced into the cell, a Kraang-droid jumped up behind us. Raph slammed the door shut on the droid's arm, tearing it from its socket. He slipped the robot arm through the door handles to keep any more Kraang-droids from joining our little party.

"That'll hold 'em," Raph said. A loud banging came from the other side of the door. "But not for long!"

The robot arm twitched and smoked. I couldn't believe what I'd just seen.

"Raph, you are seriously twisted," Leonardo said.

"Thank you," Raph said.

We took off after April and her father. We followed the winding halls out of the building and into the court-yard.

"Help!" came a cry from a walkway above.

I looked up and spotted April and her dad being hurried away by the Kraang-droids.

"Let's get them!" Leonardo shouted.

"Uh-oh," Mikey said. He looked really freaked out.

I spun around to see a giant human-weed mutant thing waving its sharp green leaves at us, ready to strike!

The **weed-man stared** down at us and growled. Actually, it was more like a hiss. Or was it a squeal? Well, whatever. He was not happy to see us.

"It's Snake!" Leonardo cried. "He's mutated into a . . . a . . . giant weed!"

Snake hissed or growled or whatever at us again.

"That's weird," Mikey said. You'd

think he'd mutate into a snake."

"Yeah, you would," Raph said to Mikey, "if you were an idiot!"

"But his name is Snake," Mikey said, explaining his own peculiar brand of logic.

"So?" Raph asked.

Mikey shook his head. "You just don't understand science."

As someone who does understand science, I just have to laugh at Mikey sometimes.

"You did this to me!" Snake hissed from the green, leafy opening that had once been his human mouth.

Technically he was right, but he did have it coming.

Snake swiped at us with a sharp, thorny vine. He knocked Mikey and Raph off their feet. Leo spun and ducked out of the way, then flashed his sword and sliced a stalk off Snake's body.

Green, gloppy goo poured out of the weed-man's wound, splashing all over Mikey.

"Ewww!" Mikey yelled. He jumped and twitched and tried to wipe off the slop.

I stared in amazement at the weed-man. The vine Leo had sliced off slowly began to grow back.

"It grew back?" I shouted. "No fair!"

The weed-man attacked us again.

In the distance I heard a faint sound. It was kind of familiar, like something I had heard before on TV, but I couldn't quite place it.

Some sort of machine was making a THAP-THAP-THAP-THAP noise.

Leo knew what it was right away.

"Donnie!" he shouted, pointing in the direction of the sound. "Go!"

There was no time to hesitate. I sprinted toward the sound, leaving my brothers to battle the weed-man.

"Snakeweed is really hard to kill!" I heard Mikey say.

"Snakeweed?" Raph asked.

"Yeah!" Mikey replied. "His name was Snake and now he's a weed, so—"

"We get it! Just keep fighting!" Raph shouted.

"We just have to hold it off until Donnie gets back!" I heard Leo say.

The pressure was squarely on me.

I rounded a bend and saw what was making the noise. It was a helicopter. Its blades spun around and around, faster and faster. Then I spotted them—April and her dad being forced into the helicopter by a group of Kraang-droids.

The helicopter started to lift off the ground. No! I had to do something.

Thinking fast, I used my *bo* staff like a pole vault to launch myself into the air.

I landed on one of the helicopter's long metal skids and hung on for dear life as it rose into the sky.

In the courtyard below, I saw my brothers battling Snakeweed. Suddenly Leo broke away from the others and ran across the roof. I wondered where he was headed. Than I saw it. He was racing to the power generator at the end of all those conduits. Way to go, Leo!

Just then, the door to the helicopter slid open and a Kraang-droid leaned out. It aimed its energy weapon at me and started blasting away.

I had to move quickly. I dodged the energy blasts, using the skid as a shield. The Kraang-droid leaned out farther. He was trying to get a better angle for a shot at me. That was when I remembered something Splinter had taught us.

He told us to always use our opponent's movement and position against him. My next move was obvious.

I reached up, grabbed the Kraang-droid's wrist, and yanked hard. He came tumbling out of the helicopter to the ground below.

However, as a scientist, I should have remembered that every action has an equal and opposite reaction. The sudden change in weight caused the helicopter to lurch to the side. April fell out the open door.

"*Yiiiiii!*" she screamed, grabbing the metal skid.

"Hold on! I'm coming!" I shouted.

But April lost her grip and plummeted toward the ground!

I don't remember thinking anything in particular. I just remember knowing that I couldn't lose her. And I knew exactly what I had to do.

I let go of the skid and dropped to the ground, using all my ninja training to land safely. I hit the ground a split second before April. Rolling up to my feet, I reached out and caught her in my arms.

"You okay?" I asked as she tried to catch her breath.

She stared up at me and nodded. Then her eyes opened wide and she looked up at the helicopter, which still held her father, as it sped off into the sky.

I felt really bad for her. I wished I could have saved her dad, too!

April and I stepped out into the court-yard. Across the way I saw Raph and Mikey hacking away at Snakeweed's leafy limbs. Then I spotted a platoon of Kraang-droids marching toward my brothers, firing their energy weapons.

Something weird was going on here. Raph and Mikey were pushing Snakeweed toward the power generator where Leo waited.

"What are they doing?" I wondered. "They're leading Snakeweed right to the power generator! That's really dangerous— and incredibly stupid!" If one of those Kraang-droid energy blasts were to hit the generator—KA-BOOM!

Or maybe . . .

"Or it's incredibly brilliant!" I said to April, who was looking at me like I had just landed from outer space. "Or it's both!"

I watched as Snakeweed came closer and closer to Leonardo, who stood just a few feet from the generator.

"Come and get me, Stinkweed!" Leo taunted.

Snakeweed raised itself up to its full height, reached back with a sharp viney tentacle, and brought it down right toward Leo's head.

But my brother was ready.

Leo did a backflip and landed directly on top of the generator. Then Leo made funny faces at the Kraang-droids.

At that moment I understood Leo's plan. It was brilliant after all.

The Kraang-droids opened fire on Leo, who jumped off the power generator just in time.

The Kraang-droids' energy blasts slammed into the generator. Powerful bolts of electricity shot from the power source and wrapped around Snakeweed.

Snakeweed went up in a shower of sparks and flames. He shrieked hideously, then collapsed in a heap of burnt plant pieces.

"Turtles, move!" Leo shouted.

The fire and smoke gave us the cover we needed to get the heck out of there!

My brothers and I, along with April, ran from the hideout.

As I left the building, I overheard the Kraang-droids talking.

"Kraang, the ones in this place are not in this place where they were," said one Kraang-droid.

"The ones are called Turtles, Kraang,"

said another. "They are dangerous to what we are doing in this place. And other places."

"Yes, I am knowledge of that," said the first. "The Turtles must be eliminated from all places."

With all that sophisticated robotic technology, you'd think they'd have better vocal-processing software, right? I don't know why they needed so many words to say they were going to get rid of us. But I did know one thing: we had made our first deadly enemies.

Once we got away from the Kraang-droid's hideout, I asked April where she planned to go, since her father was still a prisoner. She explained that her aunt lived in the city and that they were very close.

And so we went with April to her aunt's apartment.

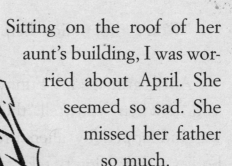

Sitting on the roof of her aunt's building, I was worried about April. She seemed so sad. She missed her father so much.

"Are you going to be all right?" I asked her.

"I guess," she said, shrugging. "My aunt says I can stay here as long as I want. But I'll be a lot better when I track down the creeps that took my dad."

"Won't the police help?" Leonardo asked.

April grimaced. "Funny thing," she said. "When you tell them your dad was kidnapped by alien brains in robot bodies, they don't take you all that seriously."

"I hear that," Mikey said.

I wanted so badly to be able to save the day for her. "April," I said, "I promise you we will not rest until we find him."

Raphael looked startled. "We won't?" he said, sounding genuinely surprised.

Leo elbowed Raph. "No, April. We won't," he said.

And that is why Leo, not Raph, is our leader!

"Thank you," April said, sighing. "But it's not your fight."

I reached out and took April's hand into mine.

"Yes," I said softly, "it is."

April looked into my eyes and, for the first time since we met, smiled at me.

I'm pretty sure I won't ever forget that smile. But all too soon, the moment was over.

April went back inside her aunt's apartment, and my brothers and I climbed down off the roof and disappeared into the darkness.

We went back to our lair. Mikey, Raph, and I flipped on the TV and settled in to relax after our big adventure. I felt glad that we had finally gotten out of the lair and into the world. But I was still worried about April.

Leonardo went to meet in private with Master Splinter. I guess that's what happens when you're the leader. But I really

wanted to know what they were saying, in case it had to do with April. So don't tell Leo, but I did a little eavesdropping with a nifty gizmo I had made out of some spare electronics.

"I am impressed, Leonardo," Splinter was saying. "You proved to be an effective leader under the most difficult of circumstances."

"Thank you, Sensei," Leo said. "And I think I figured out why you made me leader."

"Oh? Why is that?" Splinter asked.

"Because you sensed inside me a true warrior's spirit that could forge us all into the heroes we are destined to become." Leonardo was sounding pretty full of himself.

"No," Splinter replied.

"No?" Leo asked. "Then why did you make me leader?"

"Because you asked."

"That's it?" Leo said. Now he was sounding like someone had stuck a pin in his balloon. "But you seemed so certain you were right."

"As a leader, you will learn that there is no right or wrong," Splinter explained. "Only choices."

"So you could have chosen any of us?" Leo asked in a sad little voice.

"Yes."

"Even Mikey?"

"No, that would have been wrong," Splinter said quickly.

Just then, Mikey called us all over to the television set.

"Everybody! Come here!" he shouted.

"We made the news! We're on TV!"

Splinter and Leo joined us in the common area.

"There has been a report of—get this—ninjas in New York," the newscaster was saying. "Don't believe me? After residents reported a disturbance, the police recovered this."

The screen showed a picture of one of our ninja throwing stars!

"This is so awesome!" Mikey cried. "We are gonna be famous!"

Splinter scowled. Then he spoke. "You must be more careful!" he said sternly.

Whoa! I didn't expect that. He seemed kind of upset with us.

"The ninja's most powerful weapon is the shadows," he explained. "Being brought out into the light is a dangerous thing."

"Relax, Sensei," Raphael said. "It's one little news story. What's the worst that can happen?"

I wondered. What is the worst that can happen?

I guess we all should have been worried. After all, there was an army of alien robots mad at us and we were in danger of being revealed on the news. But I had to admit, I was feeling pretty good.

I almost, sort of had a girlfriend. And even more amazing, my brothers and I were really awesome ninjas. We weren't just playing in our rooms anymore. We'd been on a real mission and kicked some serious bot.

I knew I'd do anything for my brothers, and I was sure they'd always watch my shell.

We were a truly epic team!

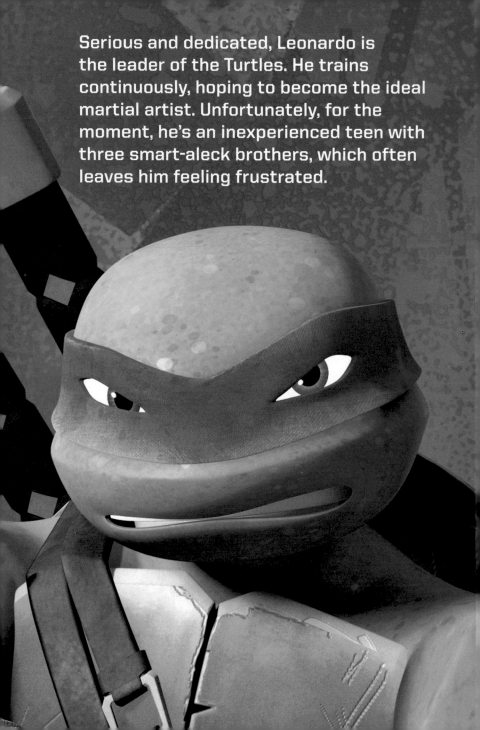

Serious and dedicated, Leonardo is the leader of the Turtles. He trains continuously, hoping to become the ideal martial artist. Unfortunately, for the moment, he's an inexperienced teen with three smart-aleck brothers, which often leaves him feeling frustrated.

NITEN RYU

Leonardo is skilled with his *katanas*, which are sharp, finely crafted steel swords. He can wield two at the same time as if they are one blade.

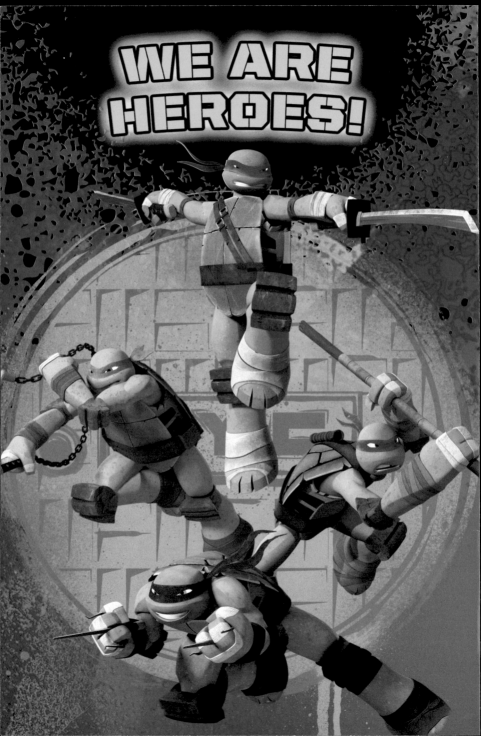

"I COULDN'T
LET THEM
GO INTO BATTLE
WITHOUT ME!"

Published in the United States by Random House Children's Books,
a division of Random House, Inc., 1745 Broadway, New York, NY 10019,
and in Canada by Random House of Canada Limited, Toronto.
Random House and the colophon are registered trademarks of
Random House, Inc. Nickelodeon, Teenage Mutant Ninja Turtles,
and all related titles, logos, and characters are trademarks of
Viacom International Inc. and Viacom Overseas Holdings C.V.
Based on characters created by Peter Laird and Kevin Eastman.

randomhouse.com/kids

ISBN: 978-0-449-80993-8

Printed in the United States of America
10 9 8 7 6 5 4 3 2 1

MUTANT ORIGIN: LEONARDO

Adapted by Michael Teitelbaum

Based on the teleplay "Day One, Part Two"
by Joshua Sternin and Jeffrey Ventimilia

RANDOM HOUSE 🏠 NEW YORK

CHAPTER 1

My name is Leonardo, and I am a turtle.

Fifteen years ago, my three brothers—Donatello, Michelangelo, and Raphael—and I were exposed to some green gooey stuff that made us change—bigtime! We mutated from tiny round turtles into human-sized turtles with human-level intelligence. Well, most of us, anyway.

Our teacher, our ninja sensei, Splinter, also changed. He used to be a human. But the same stuff that changed us also splashed on him and combined his DNA with rat DNA. So now he's a human-sized rat of extraordinary intelligence. His ninja skills are pretty amazing, too!

Splinter is like a father to me and my brothers. He raised us and trained us. Everything we know, everything we are, we owe to him.

We all live in an underground lair. It's hidden in the dark sewer tunnels deep beneath the streets of New York City. Until recently, that lair was the only world we've ever known. My brothers and I always wanted to go aboveground, but Splinter never thought it was safe. He didn't want us to go until we were ready and could

handle ourselves. We figured he was right—giant mutant turtles would probably freak people out. Who knew what they'd do to us?

Living in a sewer might sound creepy, but our lair is really awesome. We each have our own room, and Donnie even has a laboratory. He's a scientific genius and can build anything out of bits and pieces of junk. If we need a new weapon or a car, he can do it.

We also have a massive *dojo,* which is where we learn ninja fighting skills from Splinter and practice them against each other. My specialty is the *katana*—the ninja fighting sword. I can wield two at a time!

I could stay in the *dojo* all day, training

and becoming a stronger ninja, but
sometimes you need to relax. That's
why we also have a giant common

room—or what my brother Michelangelo calls our Turtle Cave. It's an epic hangout spot. We can skateboard in there or play video games. Sometimes we just kick back and watch TV, including the greatest program ever made—*Space Heroes,* the adventures of the brave crew of the space cruiser *Dauntless.* My brothers and I learned everything we know about the world from watching TV.

Sure, it's great underground, but it was still seriously exciting when Sensei finally said we could go explore the surface. I wanted to run right for the door, but stayed cool and listened as he told us not to be seen and not talk to strangers and be careful crossing streets. We promised everything would be okay.

Then Sensei let us go.

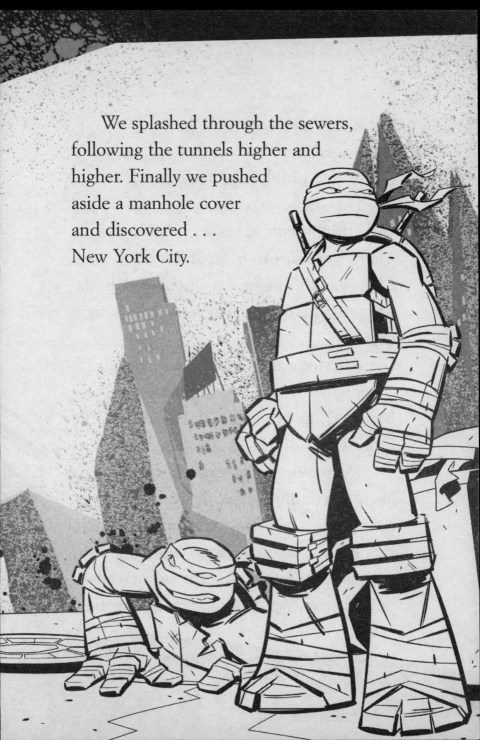

We splashed through the sewers, following the tunnels higher and higher. Finally we pushed aside a manhole cover and discovered . . . New York City.

It was dirty.

It was noisy.

It was completely amazing!

The alleys were dark, but the streets were bright with lights and flashing signs. There were surprises around every corner. That was the night we discovered pizza, which is the most insanely delicious food ever.

The city was like one giant martial arts training course. We swung from signs and bounded up buildings, then sprang from roof to roof. It was a ninja paradise!

We explored for hours, but it only felt like a few minutes. Suddenly, the sun was rising, and it was time to return to the lair. I didn't want to go back so soon, but we'd promised Splinter. I knew if we messed up on our first trip, it might be a long time

before there was another one.

I told the guys we had to head home.

That was when strange things started to happen.

Donnie peeked over a rooftop and spotted two humans walking down the street. One of them was a pretty teenage girl. It took Donnie about three seconds to fall head over heels in love with her. Which meant he was in big trouble—and so were the rest of us.

Then a van pulled up, and a bunch of men jumped out and tried to kidnap the girl and the man with her!

My brother Raphael is a great fighter, but he is also a total hothead. So naturally, he wanted to jump right in and fight off the bad guys.

Splinter had specifically told us that when we were on the surface, we had to stay away from people. But when I tried to remind Raphael of this little fact, he didn't want to hear about it. And then Donnie got all riled up, too, and he let his crush on the pretty girl cloud his judgment.

Don't get me wrong: Donatello is supersmart. He probably has the highest IQ of us all. When it comes to technical knowledge, Donnie is the man. But being smart and having basic common sense don't always go hand in hand. Donnie leaped off the rooftop to try to help the girl and her father. That was all the other guys needed. Raphael and Michelangelo followed Donnie down to the street.

I tried to convince them to come back up and go home, but they wouldn't

listen. And even though I knew getting involved was dangerous, I also knew I couldn't let

them go into battle without me. I followed them.

It was a complete disaster!

We were like four ninjas who had never met before. With every Turtle working for himself, we probably did more damage to ourselves than our enemies did. Raph almost took me out with his *sais*— two thin daggers with supersharp points— and Donnie whacked Mikey with his *bo* staff.

Even I wasn't able to score that many hits on the bad guys with those three clowns getting in my way!

Still, Donnie was just about to rescue the girl, but then Mikey crashed into him, knocking him down. So the kidnappers shoved the humans into the van and sped away.

Donnie was furious with Mikey. Raphael, Donatello, and I took off after the van, hoping we could pull off a daring rescue. Well, that failed, too. And when we got back, Mikey was ranting about big pink brains inside alien-robot bodies. We were all pretty mad and tired by then, so of course we figured Mikey was just being Mikey.

You see, Mikey is—how shall I put this?—a goofball. I mean, he'd give you the shell off his back if you needed it. He's a sweet guy. And I have to admit, he makes us all laugh. But Mikey's not the sharpest tool in the shed. That's why we gave him a hard time about the alien story. I felt kind of bad about that later on. . . .

We all went back to the lair feeling totally bummed out.

Splinter was so disappointed in us. And, you know, that hurt much worse than the defeat itself.

At first Sensei was going to ban us from going back up to the surface for a full year! I couldn't believe it. I stayed quiet, but Donnie sure didn't. He begged Sensei, saying we couldn't wait that long and had to save the girl right away.

Sensei thought deeply for a moment. He studied an old photo that showed him with his family back in Japan—a family he had lost.

Then he agreed to let us return to rescue the girl. However, he told us, this time, we had to work as a team.

And a team needed a leader.

I couldn't have agreed more.

While my brothers were fighting about

who should be chosen, I put up my hand.

"Can I be the leader?" I asked.

Splinter said yes.

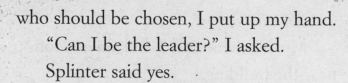

Being the leader is a big responsibility, and I take it seriously. I immediately started working on a plan to rescue the girl and her father. There was a building that had the same logo as the van that the kidnappers drove. I figured that all we had to do was go to that building and wait, and they would show up.

This time we weren't going to mess up . . . I hoped.

We returned to the city and moved through the streets, staying in the shadows and keeping quiet. We were in total stealth mode.

No one saw us.

My brothers and I hid on a rooftop near the building.

We waited and waited. This gave Raphael and Donnie a lot of time to bug me about the plan being boring and not really working. I didn't let this get to me, especially because I knew Donnie was still unhappy about not being chosen leader. On the upside, the extra time allowed me to go over the plan with Mikey again . . . and again. Sometimes he needs a little help with the details.

Finally, the van arrived.

I wanted to give them a pep talk before going into battle, because that's what leaders do. I thought of something Captain Ryan would say on *Space Heroes,* and in a deep, serious voice I announced . . .

"Men, I have a bold and daring plan! My orders must be followed precisely and—"

But my brothers had already sprung into action.

I climbed down the building after them.

We jumped down to the street and cornered the driver. He had some sort of energy blaster and fired two pulses. I back-flipped out of the way. This gave him just

enough time to get in the van and drive away. We chased after the van, springing from the lampposts and fire escapes.

Then, just as he screeched around a corner, I hurled a *shuriken*—that's a throwing star—into one of the van's tires. It exploded and the van crashed. We raced around to the front of the van. The driver was unconscious. He was a pretty creepy little guy. He had stringy hair and a mean face.

Raphael ran to the back of the van and ripped open the door. There was no one inside, but a canister fell out and rolled on the ground.

We all recognized that canister.

Splinter had shown us one just like it back in our lair. He had kept that can-

ister for fifteen years because it had an important connection to our past. It had once held the green goo that caused us all to mutate!

CHAPTER 2

We stood behind the van. Donatello pried open the canister and we all stared at the glowing green ooze inside.

"So that's it," I said. "That's the . . . the . . ."

"The mutagen that turned us into what we are now," Donatello explained.

We stood silently for a moment, and then Mikey spoke up.

"Let's drink some!" he said enthusiastically, rubbing his hands together and smacking his lips.

"What?" Raphael shouted. "Why would you do that?"

"'Cause if you mutate a mutant, you get a *super*mutant!" Mikey said it like it was totally obvious. That's how his brain works.

"Or you get a pile of goo on the sidewalk that used to be us," Donnie pointed out.

Raphael shook his head. "Either way it's an improvement," he mumbled.

As usual, I was the only one thinking about all the angles.

"Guys, this is a huge discovery," I said. "Whoever kidnapped those people is somehow connected to what happened to

us and Master Splinter fifteen years ago."

I couldn't believe it. We were about to find out what exactly had changed us and who was responsible!

"How is that possible?" Donnie asked.

"Donnie, for alien robots with brains in their stomachs, anything is possible," Mikey replied.

"Stop that!" Donatello shouted. "There's no such thing as alien robots!"

"Oh, yeah?" Mikey shouted back, walking over to the slimy little guy who had been driving the van and was now lying unconscious on the ground. "Well, if there's no such thing as alien robots, how do you explain . . . *this!*

Mikey grabbed the creepy dude's face and start to pull on it . . . hard!

The guy jolted awake from the pain.

"Ah! My face!" he yelled.

Mikey pulled on the guy's face again. And the guy screamed again.

"Man, this mask is glued on tight!" said Mikey as he kept on yanking.

Like I said, not the sharpest tool in the shed.

"Mikey, stop!" I shouted. "It's not a mask! It's the guy's face!"

Mikey finally stopped pulling.

"Okay," Mikey said. "*He's* in the clear. He's human. But those other guys . . . they were *totally* alien robots!"

Raphael shoved Mikey aside and grabbed the creepy little guy.

"Enough!" Raphael shouted. "Time to get some answers."

He got right up in the guy's face. Make no mistake, Raph is a right-up-in-your-face

kinda guy. "Who are you and what's going on?" he demanded.

The little guy sneered at Raphael. I sort of have to give him credit: he didn't show any sign that he was scared.

"Name's Snake," he snarled. "And I got nothing to say to you hideous freaks."

A grin that I can only describe as scary spread across Raphael's face.

"That's 'cause you don't know us yet," he said. Then he shoved Snake toward Mikey and Donnie. They caught him and pinned him to the ground.

Raphael picked up the canister of mutagen that had rolled out of the van. He knelt down over Snake's face and held out the canister. My brother can be pretty intimidating when he wants to be . . .

which, come to think of it, is most of the time.

"You see," Raph began, "we were just regular guys until we got hit with a little of this."

Raph started to tilt the open top of the canister toward Snake's head.

"What are you doing?" Snake screamed.

"I'm playing a little game that I like to call Mutation Roulette," Raph explained menacingly. He menaces just as well as he intimidates. He tipped the canister a little bit farther. "You could turn out handsome like me, or you might end up disgusting and deformed. Like Mikey here."

"Hey!" Mikey shouted.

Even I had to laugh at that one.

"So," Raph went on, tipping the can-

ister a little farther still, "the question you have to ask yourself is . . . do I feel lucky today?"

Raph kept tipping the canister until a tiny drop of glowing green goo formed at the edge of the open top.

It hung over Snake.

Snake stared up at the drop of goo, wide-eyed. Sweat ran down his face.

Raph seemed to be enjoying watching him squirm.

The drop stretched longer and longer. It was just about to plop onto the guy's forehead.

"Okay! Okay!" Snake finally shouted. "The guys I was with call themselves the Kraang! They've been grabbing scientists from all over the city! I don't know what they want! I just drive for them!"

Raph smiled that scary smile of his again, then slowly tipped the canister back. The glowing drop slid back inside. Then he twisted the cap on.

Raphael's techniques may not come from strict ninja disciplines, but I have to admit, they can be effective.

"That worked pretty good," I said to him.

"Of course it did," Raph agreed. "Would *you* wanna look like Mikey?"

"I'm right here!" Mikey shouted at Raph.

I leaned in close to Snake.

"What do they want with scientists?" I asked. None of this made any sense to me . . . and I don't like when things don't make sense.

"I don't know!" Snake whined.

He turned his face away from mine. Raph popped open the canister again.

Snake's face got all red. "All I know is they're taking them out of the city tonight! But I don't know where."

Donatello suddenly perked up.

"This is awesome!" he said, a big smile spreading across his face. "That girl's dad is a scientist, and *I'm* a scientist! She is so gonna like me!"

The rest of us stared at Donnie. For a really smart guy, sometimes Donnie sure can be an idiot.

"I don't think you're her type," Snake said to Donnie in his nasty little voice.

It's one thing for my brothers and me to make fun of Donnie, but I'm not

going to let some total stranger get away with it.

"Where are they now?" I demanded.

"I'll show you," Snake said, getting to his feet.

Snake led us up to a rooftop overlooking the Kraang's hideout. Mikey kept an eye on Snake, while Donnie, Raphael, and I went to the edge of the roof and checked things out.

I scanned the area with my binoculars. The place looked like a fortress. There were high walls all around that were protecting a central complex of buildings. On top of one was a helicopter. There were guards everywhere. Whatever they were doing in there,

they sure didn't want anybody learning about it.

"There's got to be, like, twenty of them down there," I reported.

"And that's just the ones we can see," Donatello said.

Immediately, I started working on a plan. One that was carefully thought-out and took into account our abilities, the number of enemies, and how we could use our ninja skills most effectively.

But as usual, Raphael just dove in.

"All right!" he shouted, flashing his *sais*. "It's time for an all-you-can-beat buffet!" He started marching toward the hideout.

"We can't just rush in there!" I shouted. "We need a plan!"

"Why?" Raphael asked, looking at me

as if I had just said the dumbest thing of all time.

Donnie stepped up to Raph. "Think, you shellbrain!" he said. "There are innocent lives at stake. If we screw this up, they're all goners!"

Thank you, Donnie, for talking sense.

"Then we won't screw up!" Raph said, all overconfident and full of himself.

Mikey stepped forward like he had something to add to the conversation.

"Boy, I could sure go for some of that pizza right now, huh?" he said.

Mikey's comment was so off-the-wall we all stopped arguing and stared at him.

"What?" Mikey said. "I can't be the only one who's hungry."

I wondered, for about the millionth time, just how he managed to get anything accomplished in life.

Then I suddenly realized that something was wrong. I couldn't put my finger on it as first, but . . .

"Where's Snake?" I asked.

Mikey looked around, then looked back at me sheepishly.

He'd let Snake escape!

"Oh, jeez, guys, I'm—"

"There he is!" I cried. I'd spotted Snake on the far side of the roof, running at top speed. "Get him!"

Snake reached the edge of the roof, climbed over, and started scrambling down the metal ladder on the side of the building. My brothers and I bounded after him and leaped off the roof. We shot down the

stairs hot on his heels, but we'd lost sight of him.

Mikey and Donnie headed in one direction, while Raph and I ran in the other. We reached the end of the street and stopped in front of a bunch of metal garbage cans and Dumpsters. I looked around, but the street was empty. I still couldn't believe Mikey had taken his eyes off of Snake!

Then I noticed some movement behind one of the Dumpsters.

It was Snake. He was so close.

I wanted to grab him right then and there.

But as the new leader, I thought it was time we started using more than just brute strength. It was time to start using our heads. A better plan quickly hatched in my brain, a plan that would get us into

that Kraang hideout. And the best part was that Snake was the guy who could help make it work.

I nudged Raphael and nodded in the direction of the Dumpster. Raph saw what I had seen and nodded back. It was showtime!

"Oh, great," I grumbled. "We let him get away."

Raphael turned toward me.

"Whoa, whoa," he said. "You're the leader. That means *you* let him get away."

Good job, Raph. Although I'm pretty sure he would have said the same thing even if we weren't playacting.

"You're not helping," I said.

"I'm not trying to help," Raph replied.

"Okay, you want me to lead?" I asked. "Fine. We'll go back to the lair and gear

up. Then at midnight, we'll drive Snake's van right up to the gate. They'll think we're him, and we'll cruise right in."

"And then we bust some heads?" Raph asked, smiling.

"And then we bust some heads," I assured him.

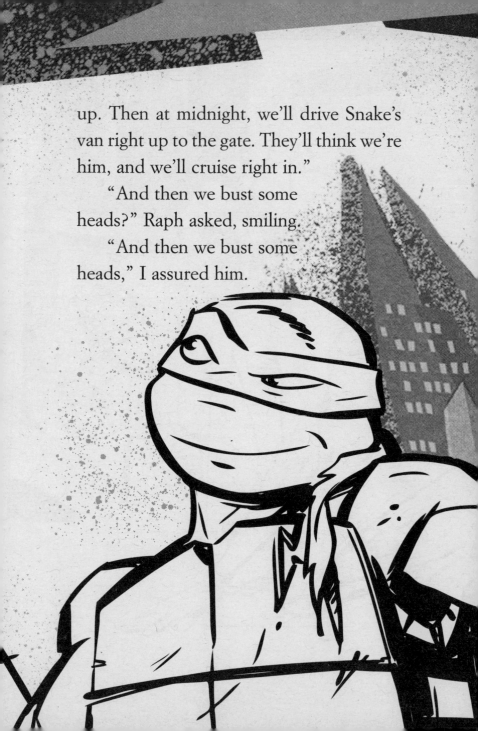

"I love a happy ending," Raph said.

We found the rest of our brothers and headed back to our lair. I knew Snake had heard everything I'd said to Raphael, and I was pretty sure he'd take the bait—right back to the Kraang.

I was feeling good about my first time as leader, but I knew we still had a long way to go.

CHAPTER 3

We rested.

We prepared.

We waited for midnight to come.

In his lab, Donnie welded together some sharp pieces of metal into tiger-claw weapons. He made some for each of us to use as we headed into our next round of combat. I don't know what Raph and Mikey were up to. They were being quiet.

A little too quiet.

Meanwhile, Splinter and I reviewed my plan of attack for that night. I was so honored that our sensei had accepted me as our leader.

I hunched over the table where we'd laid out a model of the Kraang hideout and our attack plan. It was only a couple of pencils and bolts and bottle caps, but I thought it looked good.

"I think this plan is going to work," I said, looking up at Splinter and smiling proudly.

"No plan ever survives contact with the enemy," Splinter said. "It is how you react to the unexpected that will determine if you and your brothers succeed."

Leave it to Sensei to keep things upbeat.

I had asked to be the leader, and now I was beginning to understand just what a burden that responsibility could be. I really needed a little reassurance.

"Sensei, do you think I'm ready for this?" I asked.

"Leonardo, I made you leader for a reason," Splinter explained.

Ever since Splinter had chosen me, I'd been curious why.

"What is that reason?" I asked eagerly.

"That is for you to discover on your own," Splinter replied.

Not helpful. I tried a different approach.

"There's so much riding on this," I said. "What if something goes wrong?"

Splinter stared directly into my eyes. "Failure is a possibility every leader must

face, Leonardo. It is something I had to face in Japan, in my final battle with my enemy, the Shredder."

He was more serious than I'd ever seen him before as he told me the story.

It happened when Splinter was still in human form. He was at home and Shredder struck in the night with a surprise attack. The two ninjas battled. Shredder swung his tiger claw viciously. One blow caught Splinter's face, scarring his cheek. Splinter's wife watched in terror, clutching their infant daughter.

During the fight, a candle fell and started a fire. The flames spread. They climbed the walls and flashed across the ceiling.

The roof collapsed.

Shredder ran away into the night, but Splinter wasn't able to stop him . . .

and he wasn't able to save his family.

Splinter kneeled silently in front of his burning house.

"But that's my point, Sensei," I said softly. "You lost everything."

Splinter stared at a wall. He was obviously still remembering that terrible night.

Then he looked up at me.

"I lost many things," he explained. "My family, my

home, my name. But I gained many things as well. Like the four of you."

All I wanted at that moment was to make him proud, to live up to his expectations of us.

"Don't worry, Sensei," I said. "We can handle this."

Of course, that was the moment Mikey picked to come running through the common room wearing a metal pot on his head and screaming at the top of his lungs. Raph was running after him, threatening him with a wooden spoon and shouting, "Get back here!"

Sensei and I watched them run past, and then we both sighed deeply.

We could handle this?

I sure hoped so.

CHAPTER 4

It was seconds to midnight.

Snake's van raced down an empty street—right toward the gate of the Kraang's hideout. The guards turned and fired their energy weapons.

Snake was with them, and he fired, too.

BLAM! BLAM! BLAM!

Blinding flashes lit up the night.

But the van kept coming.

Snake and the guards dove out of the
way as the van crashed into the gate and
exploded in a bright orange fireball!

A single canister of mutagen flew into
the air and landed right on Snake, cover-
ing him in green goo.

He let out a horrible scream as the chemical went to work on him.

He started to twist and grow. Snake began to change.

The Kraang ran over to the burning van and forced the door open. And that was when they discovered that the van was empty—not even a driver was inside.

And where were we?

Climbing up the side of the Kraang's building using Donnie's tiger claws. We watched all the action safely from the shadows. After Raph and I had used a little misdirection on Snake earlier that day, I had Donnie rig up an automatic driving device for Snake's van. That way the van could distract the Kraang while my brothers and I infiltrated their hideout.

I had to admit, I was really pleased.

Everything worked perfectly.

"Wow!" Mikey said as we slowly made our way up the side of the building. "Lucky thing that the van showed up to distract them."

Exasperated with Mikey being so . . . Mikey, Donnie smacked himself in the head. Unfortunately, he was wearing a tiger claw, so it really hurt.

"That was the plan all along, Mikey," I explained for the fiftieth time. "We knew Snake was hiding in the alley, so Raph and I made him think we would be in the van."

Mikey still looked confused.

"But we weren't in the van," Mikey pointed out.

Classic Mikey.

"Just keep climbing," I told him.

"Can do," Mikey replied.

We reached the top of the wall and slipped inside the compound. What we saw was unbelievable, unlike anything I'd ever seen before or could possibly imagine. The outside of the building looked perfectly normal, like an ordinary warehouse. But the inside . . .

Even Donnie the tech geek was completely blown away!

THE STORY DOESN'T END
HERE! FLIP YOUR BOOK
OVER AND LET DONATELLO
TELL YOU THE REST OF
THIS ADVENTURE!